THE OWL AND THE TWO RABBITS

Publisher's Note:
This book is based on an Inuit traditional story. The author was inspired by a version of this traditional story from the Kivalliq region of Nunavut, where she grew up. The story you are about to read is a creative retelling of this original story.

Published by Inhabit Media Inc. | www.inhabitmedia.com

Inhabit Media Inc. (Iqaluit) P.O. Box 11125, Iqaluit, Nunavut, X0A 1H0
(Toronto) 191 Eglinton Avenue East, Suite 310, Toronto, Ontario, M4P 1K1

Design and layout copyright © 2019 Inhabit Media Inc.
Text copyright © 2019 Nadia Sammurtok
Illustrations by Marcus Cutler copyright © 2019 Inhabit Media Inc.

Editors: Neil Christopher and Kelly Ward
Art Director: Danny Christopher
Designer: Astrid Arijanto

We acknowledge the support of the Canada Council for the Arts for our publishing program. This project was made possible in part by the Government of Canada.

ISBN: 978-1-77227-236-9

Printed in Canada

Library and Archives Canada Cataloguing in Publication

Title: The owl and the two rabbits / by Nadia Sammurtok ; illustrated by Marcus Cutler.
Names: Sammurtok, Nadia, author. | Cutler, Marcus, 1978- illustrator.
Identifiers: Canadiana 20190061650 | ISBN 9781772272369 (hardcover)
Classification: LCC PS8637.A5384 O95 2019 | DDC jC813/.6—dc23

THE OWL AND THE TWO RABBITS

By Nadia Sammurtok · Illustrated by Marcus Cutler

It was a beautiful, crisp evening, and two rabbit sisters had just finished their dinner. Even though their parents had told them to remain hidden when they played outside—so as not to draw the attention of predators—they decided to go play on some rocks close to a hillside.

At first the two rabbits moved slowly, careful not to draw attention to themselves. But they soon forgot about being cautious as they found some rocks to jump on.

"Watch this!" said the smaller rabbit. She jumped as high as she could, landing on top of a big boulder.

3

"Wow! That's high, Sister!" replied the bigger rabbit.
"But I bet you can't do this!"

The bigger rabbit leapt as high as she could and landed on the other side of the huge boulder.

"That's amazing!" called the smaller rabbit.

Suddenly, an owl swooped down, landing right in front of where they were standing.

6

"What's going on here?" said the owl. His huge wings spread out from left to right, completely blocking the way back to the rabbits' den. The rabbits froze with fear as they studied him from top to bottom.

The owl's sharp talons dug into the ground as he stared at the two rabbits.

In a timid voice, the bigger rabbit said, "W-w-we were just p-p-playing over here."

"I can see that, and now I'm going to take you back to my nest for dinner!" the owl roared as he closed his talons around each rabbit. The owl quickly tried to take flight, but with two rabbits in his claws, he could not get off the ground.

Terrified, the rabbits tried to free themselves from the owl's sharp talons. They pushed and pushed until they were able to get their feet on the ground.

Once the rabbits had freed their feet, they ran as fast as they could, pulling the owl behind them as they went.

As he struggled to right himself, the owl heard his wife yelling from a distance, "Let one go! We'll have the other!"

The owl called back to his wife, "No! I want both of them! Too much time will pass before we can find another and we will go hungry!"

The rabbits ran as fast and as far as they could, and the owl soon tired of holding on to them. He let go of them but continued to follow, soaring through the air just overhead.

The rabbits kept on running. They spotted a huge boulder sitting on top of a hill.

"Come on! Over to that boulder! We will run behind it and push it on top of the owl!" cried the bigger rabbit.

"We can try," said the smaller rabbit doubtfully. The boulder looked too big for them to move, but she was willing to try anything to get away from the owl.

The rabbits stopped at the boulder, one on each side, and waited for the owl to catch up.

Soon after, the owl swooped down towards them. He landed right in front of the boulder. The rabbit sisters were terrified, but they stayed where they were.

"Ah, finally . . . Now come over here and let's make this quick. I am very hungry," said the owl.

20

The bigger rabbit whispered to her sister, "Now, Sister, push as hard as you can!"

And so, the rabbits pushed the boulder with as much strength as their bodies had, and the boulder rolled quickly towards the owl.

The owl could not get away and disappeared beneath the boulder. Relieved, the rabbits jumped for joy, knowing they had defeated the hungry owl.

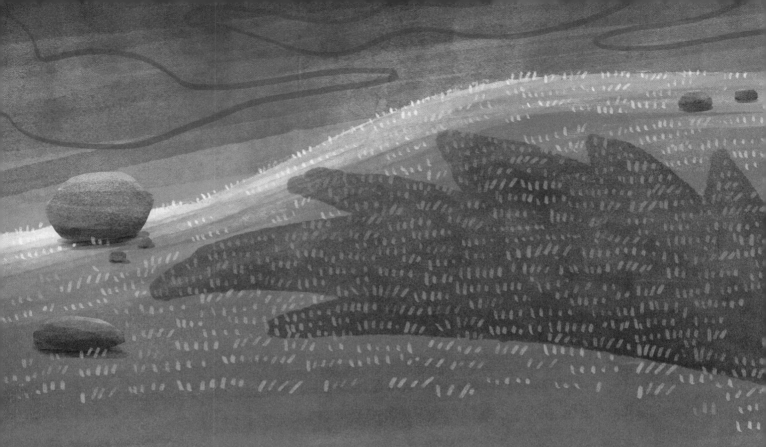

Then, worried that the owl's wife might come after them, the rabbits hid amongst some Arctic willow, staying perfectly still as she swooped past them. The rabbits' brown coats blended in with the tundra, making it hard for the female owl to see them.

As she passed, the rabbits heard her grumble, "I told him he should have gone for only one at a time. Now look what's happened."

The female owl flew away, and the two little rabbits were finally safe.

They had learned to never again play out in the open where hungry owls might find them, and they were glad they had defeated the greedy owl.

Nadia Sammurtok is an Inuit writer and educator originally from Rankin Inlet, Nunavut. Nadia is passionate about preserving the traditional Inuit lifestyle and Inuktitut language so that they may be enjoyed by future generations. Nadia currently lives in Iqaluit, Nunavut, with her family.

Marcus Cutler is a both a children's illustrator and an occasional climber of rocks. He lives and works in Windsor, Ontario, with his wife and two daughters.

INHABIT MEDIA INC.